AFTER-SCHOOL
SPORTS
CLUB
Let's Go Skating!

For M. J. L., D. C., and A. R.
—A. H.

For Linda Gross, a teacher who knows how to be
caring, goofy, fun, and wonderful
—S. B.

ALADDIN

An imprint of Simon & Schuster Children's Publishing Division

1230 Avenue of the Americas, New York, NY 10020

First Aladdin paperback edition December 2009

Text copyright © 2009 by Simon & Schuster, Inc.

Illustrations copyright © 2009 by Steve Björkman

ALADDIN is a trademark of Simon & Schuster, Inc., and related logo is

a registered trademark of Simon & Schuster, Inc.

READY-TO-READ is a registered trademark of Simon & Schuster, Inc.

For information about special discounts for bulk purchases, please contact

Simon & Schuster Special Sales at 1-866-506-1949 or business@simonandschuster.com.

The Simon & Schuster Speakers Bureau can bring authors to your live event.

For more information or to book an event contact the Simon & Schuster Speakers

Bureau at 1-866-248-3049 or visit our website at www.simonspeakers.com.

Designed by Krista Olsen

The text of this book was set in Century Schoolbook BT.

The illustrations for this book were rendered in ink and watercolor.

Manufactured in the United States of America

0715 LAK

2 4 6 8 10 9 7 5 3

Full CIP data for this book is available from the Library of Congress.

ISBN: 978-1-4169-9411-4

AFTER-SCHOOL SPORTS CLUB
Let's Go Skating!

Written by ALYSON HELLER

Illustrated by STEVE BJÖRKMAN

Ready-to-Read

ALADDIN

New York   London   Toronto   Sydney

The After-School
Sports Club was going
on a field trip.

"We are going to learn how to ice-skate," said Mr. Mac.

"And we are going to
the rink in the park!"

"Ice-skating!" said Tess.
"That sounds like fun!"

When they got to the rink,
there were lots of
people there.

The kids were all excited—
except Alyssa.

What if she fell? It looked like it would hurt—a *lot*.

"Time to rent some skates,"
said Mr. Mac.

"The skating teachers here will help us."

J.B. and Caleb got their
skates and headed to the
ice with Mr. Mac.

"Come on, Alyssa!"
yelled J.B.

"No thanks,"
Alyssa said.

Tess and Sammy got their
skates and stepped onto
the ice with a teacher
from the rink.

"Come on, Alyssa!"
Tess said. "It is lots of
fun out here!"

"I am okay," Alyssa said.

Soon Mr. Mac came by.
"Do you want
to try now, Alyssa?"

He held out his hand.
"I will skate with you,
if you want."

Alyssa watched the other
kids wobble across the ice.
They were all smiling.
It *did* look like fun.

Mr. Mac helped Alyssa
lace up her skates.
"Do not worry about
falling," he said.

Alyssa took a few small
steps on the ice.

She pushed off with
her right foot, then
her left foot.

Soon she was going
around the rink. She did
not fall once!

"That was a lot of fun,"
Alyssa said. "I cannot
wait to come back!"

"See? I knew you could do it!" said Mr. Mac.